TURTLE ISLAND

KEViN SHERRY

 Dial Books for Young Readers ✣ an imprint of Penguin Group (USA) LLC

To Elizabeth Katherine Heather King

I'd also like to thank my parents and my city, Baltimore

DIAL BOOKS FOR YOUNG READERS
Published by the Penguin Group • Penguin Group (USA) LLC
375 Hudson Street, New York, New York 10014

USA / Canada / UK / Ireland / Australia / New Zealand / India / South Africa / China
penguin.com
A Penguin Random House Company

Library of Congress Cataloging-in-Publication Data

Sherry, Kevin, author, illustrator.
Turtle Island / story and pictures by Kevin Sherry.
pages   cm
Summary: A giant turtle's loneliness ends when a boatload of animals is shipwrecked and makes a temporary home on his shell.
But when they decide to sail for home, will the turtle be alone once more?
ISBN 978-0-8037-3391-6 (hardcover)
[1. Turtles—Fiction. 2. Loneliness—Fiction. 3. Friendship—Fiction. 4. Animals—Fiction. 5. Islands—Fiction.] I. Title.
PZ7.S549Tur 2014   [E]—dc23   2013027091

Manufactured in China on acid-free paper

10 9 8 7 6 5 4 3 2 1

Designed by Jasmin Rubero
Text set in Anno 1 Corn Regular

The art was penciled, inked, then painted with watercolors.

I'm a giant turtle, and
I'm as BIG as an island.

But the ocean is even BIGGER,
and sometimes I get lonely.

So imagine my surprise
when one day . . .

I had visitors!

They were shipwrecked,
which was bad, but I could fish,
which was good!

And do you know what?

Owl could knit,
    Bear could build,

Frog could cook,

and Cat could draw.

We all worked together.

Suddenly, things were happening.

And the sea didn't seem so big anymore.

Until . . .

"We miss our families," Frog said one day.

I didn't understand. Wasn't *I* their family?

"We have to go home,"
Bear added.
But wasn't *I* their home?

Bear built a ship,

Owl knit a sail,

Frog packed some food,

and Cat . . .

Cat gave me a hug.

And they sailed away.

I was alone again.

I couldn't stop
thinking about my friends.

I tried to stay busy.
But things weren't the same.

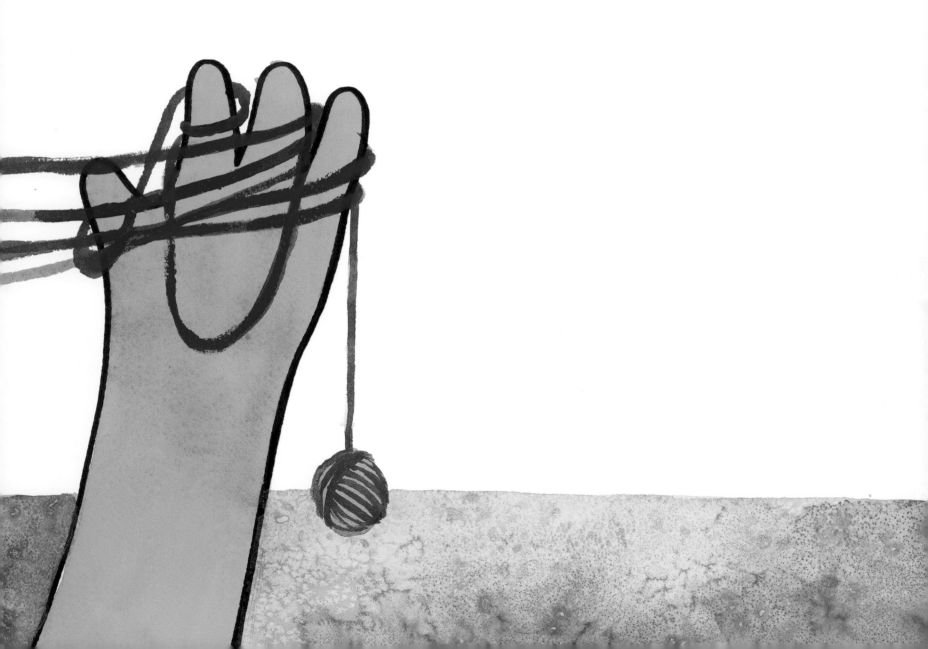

I thought I would be alone forever.

So imagine my surprise
when one day . . .

I saw a boat!

And who was in it?
My friends! And they had brought
something very special.

They had brought all of **THEIR** friends,

and their **FAMILIES** too!

This is how
Turtle Island started . . .

and how we continue to grow.